curvy girl for the cop

emma bray

one

. . .

Ryan

THE WINDING MOUNTAIN road stretches before me, an endless ribbon of asphalt leading into the heart of nowhere. I grip the steering wheel, knuckles white, jaw clenched. This "vacation" is a joke. A punishment.

Towering pines close in, their shadows casting an ominous shroud over the car. I glance at my bandaged hand, still raw from the fight that landed me here. I should be on the city streets, amidst the chaos and grit where I belong. Not exiled to some backwater town playing at finding inner peace.

The GPS dings, signaling my arrival in Pine

Hollow. I pull up to a row of rustic storefronts, their weathered facades proclaiming small-town charm. Letting out a heavy sigh, I step out, stretching my taut muscles. The mountain air chills my lungs, crisp and foreign.

My gaze lands on a cozy bookshop nestled between the hardware store and post office. Through the window, I glimpse a flash of mahogany hair, soft curves. Something stirs within me, primal and unbidden. I blink it away. I'm here to clear my head, not muddy the waters with distractions, no matter how enticing.

I let my eyes wander, taking in the quaint storefronts lining the main street. A dingy diner with a flickering 'Open' sign. The obligatory general store boasting everything from fishing tackle to homemade jam. A run-down movie theater marquee advertising titles months old.

This place is a time capsule, cut off from the rest of the world and stuck in some nostalgic past. The kind of town where everybody knows each other's business and outsiders stick out like a sore thumb. And here I am, a walking cliché—the jaded city cop looking for answers at the bottom of a bottle and the end of a winding road.

I shake my head, trying to dispel the bitter thoughts. I came here for a reason, even if it wasn't by choice. To clear the cobwebs, exorcise some demons, and maybe, just maybe, remember what it feels like to breathe again.

But damn if I can focus on any of that noble bullshit when my traitorous gaze keeps drifting back to that bookshop and the tantalizing curves I glimpsed through the window. There's something about the way she moved, an unconscious grace that spoke of quiet confidence and raw sensuality. I can almost picture tracing the slope of her hip, the dip of her waist, with calloused fingertips...

I clench my fists, feeling the sharp sting of my split knuckles. I didn't drive halfway across the state to get my head turned around by some small town librarian. I'm here to get my shit together, not fall into bed with the first attractive woman I see.

Except I can't seem to tear my eyes away from that storefront. Can't stop imagining what it would feel like to lose myself in soft flesh and honeyed sighs, to bury my demons in the welcoming heat of her body until all that's left is blessed oblivion.

"Fuck it," I mutter under my breath, propelling myself forward on leaden feet. Toward the book-shop. Toward her. Toward the inescapable gravity that draws me in like a moth to a flame, heedless of the inferno that awaits.

The bell above the door jingles cheerfully as I

step inside, announcing my arrival like a harbinger of doom. The scent of ink and paper and something uniquely feminine washes over me. My heart pounds against my ribcage as I venture further into her domain, each step a battle between desire and self-preservation.

I round a corner and there she is, all generous curves and flushed cheeks, hazel eyes widening as they meet mine. In that moment, I know I'm well and truly fucked. And I can't bring myself to care.

Ava

The bell above the door jingles and I glance up from the stack of newly arrived first editions. My breath catches. He's tall, dark, and radiating an intensity that snakes down my spine and coils in my belly.

A stranger. In my shop. In our town.

I smooth my hair, suddenly acutely aware of my generous curves straining against my corn-flower sundress. *Get it together, Ava.* I paste on my best customer service smile. "Welcome to

Dawson's Book Nook. Can I help you find anything?"

My words hang in the air between us as his eyes, the color of a gathering storm, rake over me. A muscle ticks in his chiseled jaw. The silence stretches, charged and heavy.

Finally, he clears his throat. "Just passing through. Thought I'd browse." His voice is low, rough like gravel.

"Of course, please, take your time." I gesture to the lovingly curated shelves, my sanctuary. "If you need any recommendations, I'm happy to help."

He nods, a curt jerk of his chin. Then turns and disappears into the stacks, a predator melting into the shadows. I release a shaky exhale.

Lord help me, but I want to unravel the mystery coiled within that man. Want to crack open his hard exterior and consume the pages of his story, no matter how dark.

I shake my head. I've always been drawn to the broken ones, haven't I?

My gaze strays to the "Local Authors" display. To the slim volume of poetry bearing my name. We all have our secrets. Pine Hollow may look idyllic, but it has a way of unearthing the hidden things.

The man prowls through the aisles, his presence electric, inescapable in the small shop. I try to focus on the inventory list in front of me, but the words blur together. I'm hyper-aware of every sound—the creak of a floorboard, the whisper of pages turning. The sizzle of my nerve endings.

Breathe, Ava. He's just a man.

An impossibly gorgeous, mysterious man who makes your knees weak, but still.

I'm startled from my reverie by the thud of a book on the counter. I glance up to find him looming over me, a paperback between us. His fingers drum an impatient beat on the worn wood.

"Find everything you were looking for?" I hate the tremor in my voice. *Get a grip!*

A ghost of a smile, there and gone. "Not exactly what I had in mind, but it'll do."

I ring him up on autopilot, hyper-focused on keeping my hands steady. Our fingers brush as I hand him the receipt. A jolt of awareness, a live wire.

His gaze snaps to mine, searching. I wonder if he felt it too. The crackle of connection, the swoop low in my belly. Dangerous territory.

"I'm Ryan. Ryan Callahan." An offer. Or a warning.

"Ava. Dawson. Obviously." I cringe inwardly. Real smooth.

A real smile this time, just a quirk of his lips.

"Thanks for the help, Ava Dawson. I'm sure I'll be seeing you around."

Is that a threat or a promise? He's out the door before I can decide, the bell jingling in his wake. I slump against the counter, boneless.

What the hell just happened? And why do I suddenly feel like Little Red Riding Hood who's just caught the eye of the Big Bad Wolf?

Pine Hollow just got a whole lot more interesting.

Lord help me, indeed.

———

My thoughts swirl as I close up the shop. The memory of his touch, the weight of his gaze, and the way my name sounded like a secret on his lips.

I head home, my mind abuzz with images of his dark hair, his tall frame.

Those eyes that seemed to see right through me…

I settle into my cozy couch, book untouched on my lap. The fire crackles, but it's no match for the flames his presence ignited within me.

I can't afford to fall for another city boy, I remind myself. I can control my wayward heart. I have to.

But as I drift off to sleep, the contours of Ryan's

face linger in my dreams, and I wonder if I'm already too late.

The fire in the hearth crackles, casting shadows that dance across the walls of my cozy cottage. In my mind's eye, I see him again, standing in my shop, leaning over the counter as if he were about to devour me whole. The heat between us had been palpable, the tension thick enough to slice with a knife.

I blush, remembering how my heart had raced when he'd looked at me. Heat pools between my thighs as I replay our conversation in my mind. His smirk, his confidence, the way his shirt had clung to his chest, accentuating every rippling muscle.

Restless, I toss and turn, unable to banish the memory of his eyes from my thoughts.

two

. . .

Ryan

DAMN, there's something about her.

Ava Dawson, the curvy, shy-but-not-really bookstore owner. She's different from the women I'm used to. No airs, no games. Just a girl who knows her books and has curves in all the right places.

My mind's in the gutter, but I can't help it. Last thing I need is to complicate my life, but the pull is there, like a magnetic force.

I refused to allow myself to go back to the bookstore today.

Still, I can't shake her from my thoughts.

I tell myself she's off-limits. I'm just passing through, and she deserves more than a fling.

But when my Jeep decides to cough its last on a deserted backroad, of course, she's the one to give me a lift.

Her car is a confined space, filled with the scent of books and sun-warmed leather. Her hair falls in a cascade of chestnut, and my fingers itch to unravel her braid.

We drive in silence, interrupted only by the soft purr of the engine and my own ragged breathing. The tension is thick, like the charged air before a storm.

I look over at her and my cock hardens in my pants.

Fuck, I've got it bad.

Ava

The car ride stretches out before us, an endless ribbon of road winding through the pines. I steal glances at Ryan from the corner of my eye, tracing the strong line of his jaw, the way his hands grip his thighs. Those hands...

"So, what brought you to Pine Hollow?" My voice shatters the silence, too loud in the confines of the car.

Ryan's eyes flick to mine, then back to the road. "Needed a change of scenery. Someplace quiet to clear my head."

I nod, sensing the weight behind his words. "The mountains have a way of doing that. Putting things in perspective."

"What about you?" he asks, genuine curiosity threading his tone. "Have you always lived here?"

"Born and raised." I smile, a bittersweet tug. "I left for college, but the mountains called me home. There's nowhere else I'd rather be."

His gaze lingers on my face, searching. "Must be nice, having roots like that. Knowing where you belong."

The wistfulness in his voice catches me off guard. I wonder what it would be like, to be untethered. Free to roam. The thought sends a shiver down my spine.

We lapse into silence, but it's different now. Charged. I'm acutely aware of every shift of his body, every breath. The heat of him seeps into my skin, settling deep in my bones.

Too soon, we're pulling up to his rental cabin. I put the car in park, my hands trembling slightly on the wheel. This is it. The end of the line.

Ryan makes no move to get out, his eyes locked on mine. The air between us crackles with unspoken words, unacknowledged desires. I'm drawn to him like a moth to a flame, reckless and inevitable.

"Ava..." His voice is low, rough. A caress and a question.

I swallow hard, my heart a wild thing in my chest. "Yes?"

His hand covers mine on the gearshift, calluses rasping against my skin. I suck in a sharp breath, every nerve ending sparking to life.

"Thank you. For the ride." His thumb strokes the delicate bones of my wrist, a whisper of a touch. "And the company."

I nod, not trusting my voice. He lingers a moment longer, his gaze searing into mine. A promise. A challenge. Then he's gone, the car door slamming shut behind him.

I watch him walk away, his broad shoulders disappearing into the gathering dusk. My body thrums with unspent energy, a livewire of longing.

What is it about this man that unravels me so completely? That leaves me aching and raw, desperate for more?

I close my eyes, resting my forehead against the steering wheel. I'm in trouble. Deep, delicious trouble.

three

. . .

Ryan

THE BELL above the door jingles as I step into the cozy bookshop, warmth enveloping me. Ava glances up from the counter, her eyes widening slightly before a soft smile graces her lips. As if drawn by an invisible force, my feet carry me towards her.

"Well, look who's back," she says, tucking a stray lock of hair behind her ear. "Did you forget something last time?"

I lean against the counter, flashing her a crooked grin. I don't know what the hell I'm doing, but I can't seem to stop myself. "Just couldn't stay away from your charming company, I suppose."

My eyes linger on the delicate flush creeping up her neck. The urge to trace its path with my fingertips is almost overwhelming.

Ava raises an eyebrow, a glimmer of mischief in her eyes. "Is that so? And here I thought you were just here for the books."

"Oh, the books are a definite perk. But I have to admit, the banter is even more enticing."

She laughs softly, the sound sending a pleasant shiver down my spine. "Careful there, you might make a girl think you're flirting with her."

"Would that be such a bad thing?" The words slip out before I can stop them.

A beat of silence stretches between us as Ava holds my gaze. Anticipation coils in my gut, mingling with the simmering attraction that grows stronger each time we meet.

"I suppose not," she finally murmurs, her voice barely above a whisper. "But you know what they say about playing with fire..."

"Sometimes the risk is worth the reward, don't you think?"

I know I'm treading on dangerous ground, blurring the lines between casual acquaintances and something more. But with Ava, I can't seem to help myself. She awakens a desire I thought long buried.

Her tongue darts out to wet her lips, and I find myself mirroring the action. The air between us crackles with unspoken tension, a dance of push and pull that leaves me aching for more.

My gaze trails over her curves, appreciating the way her soft sweater clings to her enticing figure. She shifts under my appraisal, a delicate flush creeping up her neck. I wonder if her skin would feel as smooth as it looks, if her pulse would race beneath my fingertips.

Ava clears her throat, breaking the charged silence. "Did you, um, need help finding anything specific today?"

"Actually, I was hoping you could recommend something." I step closer, drawn to her. "Something that might surprise me."

Her eyes widen slightly, but she doesn't back away. "I think I might have just the thing."

She turns, leading me deeper into the store. I follow, admiring the sway of her hips and the way her dark hair cascades down her back. She stops at a shelf, her fingers skimming over the spines until she plucks out a worn paperback.

"Here, try this one." She holds it out to me, our fingers grazing as I take it from her hand.

Electricity arcs between us at the brief contact, sending a jolt straight to my core. Ava inhales sharply, her lips parting in surprise. I fight the urge to pull her close, to crush my mouth against hers and taste her sweetness.

"Thanks," I manage, my voice rougher than intended. "I trust your judgment."

"You shouldn't." The words are barely audible, but I catch them nonetheless.

"And why is that?" I lean in, invading her space, breathing in her scent of vanilla and old books.

She tilts her head back, her eyes darkening with an emotion I can't quite place. "Because you don't know me, Ryan. Not really."

"But I want to." The confession hangs between us, raw and honest. "I want to know everything about you, Ava."

Her breath hitches, her chest rising and falling rapidly. I can practically feel the heat radiating off her skin, the tension coiling tighter with each passing second.

"I'm not sure that's a good idea," she whispers, but there's a yearning in her tone that belies her words.

"Let me be the judge of that." I raise my hand, slowly, giving her time to pull away. When she doesn't, I brush a stray lock of hair behind her ear, my knuckles grazing her cheek. "I'm willing to take the risk, if you are."

Ava's eyes flutter closed at my touch, a shaky exhale escaping her lips. I can sense her internal struggle, the warring desires within her. I know I should step back, give her space, but I'm captivated by the way she responds to me.

"Ryan..." My name falls from her lips like a prayer and a plea all at once.

"Tell me to stop, and I will." My thumb traces the delicate line of her jaw, marveling at the softness of her skin. "Just say the word, Ava."

Her eyes open, meeting mine with an intensity that steals my breath. In that moment, I know I'm lost. I'll gladly drown in the depths of her gaze, surrender to the fire she ignites within me.

The world narrows to just the two of us, poised on the brink of something dangerous and exhilarating. The air hums with possibility, and I can almost taste the sweetness of her lips, feel the curves of her body pressed against mine.

But the decision is hers. I'll only take what she's willing to give, even if it means walking away with nothing more than the memory of this moment.

So I wait, my heart pounding in my chest, as Ava weighs the consequences of giving in to the desire that burns between us.

Her decision will change everything.

Ava's lips part, a shaky exhale escaping as her tongue darts out to moisten them. My gaze is drawn to the movement, transfixed by the glossy sheen it leaves behind. I imagine capturing that lush mouth with my own, tasting her sweetness, drinking in her sighs of pleasure.

She sways closer, and I feel the heat of her body radiating through the scant space between us. It takes every ounce of my restraint not to haul her against me, to let my hands roam over her soft curves until she's trembling with need.

"Ryan, I..." Her voice wavers, uncertainty warring with longing in her eyes. "We shouldn't. This isn't...I'm not..."

I silence her protests with a gentle brush of my thumb over her plump lower lip. "Shh, it's okay. We don't have to do anything you're not ready for."

Even as the words leave my mouth, I know I'm teetering on the edge of my control. The primal, possessive part of me wants to lay claim to her, to brand her as mine until there's no doubt in her mind that she belongs with me.

But I won't push. I'll let Ava set the pace, even if it means enduring the sweetest kind of torture as I wait for her to decide what she wants.

Her teeth sink into her lip, worrying the tender

flesh as she searches my face. I wonder what she sees there. Does she glimpse the hunger I'm barely keeping in check? The dark promise of pleasure I long to fulfill?

"Kiss me." The words are barely a whisper, but they ring out like a clarion call in the charged silence.

I don't hesitate. Cupping her face in my hands, I lower my mouth to hers, finally taking what I've craved since the moment I first laid eyes on her.

Her lips are soft and yielding beneath mine, parting on a gasp as I slant my mouth over hers. I lick into her, savoring her unique flavor—sweet with a hint of innocence that makes me want to corrupt her in the most delicious ways.

Ava melts against me, her curvy body molding to my harder planes as her arms wind around my neck. She meets me stroke for stroke, giving as good as she gets. It's intoxicating, the way she responds so passionately, so uninhibitedly. As if she's been waiting for this—for me.

A part of me knows we're moving too fast, that this is crazy, we just met, that we're hurtling towards something neither of us may be prepared for. But with Ava in my arms, her tongue tangling with mine as our kiss turns deeper, *hungrier*, I can't bring myself to care.

All I want is to lose myself in her, to make her mine in every way that matters. And from the needy little moans she's making, the way her nails bite into my shoulders, I'd say she wants the same.

It won't be gentle. It won't be sweet. But it will be unforgettable.

Suddenly, Ava pulls back, her chest heaving as she stares up at me with eyes clouded with desire. "Ryan... we need to stop."

"Why?" I growl, my voice raw with arousal. "We both know you want this." I take her hand and press it against my erection, making sure she can feel just how hard she makes me.

Ava gasps, her cheeks flushing a deep crimson, but she doesn't remove her hand. Instead, she digs her nails in slightly, as if she's as torn as I am.

In the end, however, she's the one with enough strength to break our connection. "Because...because I'm scared."

Scared? Of me? The thought sends a jolt of possessiveness through me. "You have nothing to be scared of, baby. I'd never hurt you."

Ava bites her lower lip, her eyes welling up with unshed tears. "I know...it's not that I'm scared of you... it's..."

"Then what?" I prod, my voice gentler now. I

want to help her, to rid her of whatever ghosts are holding her back.

"I'm scared of myself," she whispers. "I've never felt this way about anyone before, and it's crazy cause it's too fast, I'm terrified of getting my heart broken again."

Wait…again?

I almost see red at the thought of another man touching her.

"Who broke your heart?" I bark out.

She jumps at my voice, and I work to lower my volume. "Who hurt you, sweetheart?"

She bites her lip before she shakes her head. "I mean, I guess it's silly. Although we called ourselves 'boyfriend and girlfriend,' we never really did anything except kiss."

My shoulders relax only to tense back up again. She didn't do anything other than kiss, so I don't have to imagine another man inside her, but she did kiss, so now I have deal with the thought of another man's lips on her.

I can't quite contain the growl that rumbles up out of my chest at that thought.

Ava looks up at me with wide eyes, startled by the possessive sound emanating from deep within me. "Ryan?" she whispers uncertainly.

I take a deep breath, trying to rein in the jealousy swirling inside me at the thought of her with someone else, even if it was just kissing. I have no right to feel this way, but the primal part of me wants to erase any trace of another man's touch from her mind, her body.

"I'm sorry," I murmur, cupping her face gently. "I just...I don't like the thought of anyone hurting you. Of anyone else touching you."

Her breath hitches at my confession, her pupils dilating with renewed desire. "I've never been touched...not really. Not the way I want you to touch me."

Fuck. Her innocent admission nearly undoes me. I lean in, my lips brushing the shell of her ear as I whisper roughly, "Tell me how you want me to touch you, Ava. Tell me what you need."

She shivers, her hands fisting in my shirt. "I...I want your hands on me. Everywhere. I want you to make me forget everything except how you feel."

A low growl escapes me at her breathy plea. "I can do that, baby. I'll make you forget your own name by the time I'm done with you."

Ava whimpers, arching into me as if she can't get close enough. I slide my hand into her hair, tugging gently until she bares her throat to me. Trailing open-mouthed kisses along the slender column, I nip and suck at her fluttering pulse, marking her as mine.

"Ryan, please..." She's panting now, her hips undulating against my thigh, seeking friction.

"Please what? Use your words, sweet girl." I scrape my teeth over her collarbone, soothing the sting with my tongue.

"Touch me," she begs. "I need your hands on my skin. I need you."

Satisfaction hums through me at her wanton plea. "Then let's get you out of these clothes. I want to see all of you, touch all of you."

Ava nods frantically, already tugging at the hem of her sweater. Together, we strip her bare, until she's standing before me in nothing but a pair of pale pink panties.

My hungry gaze rakes over her curves, committing every dip and swell to memory. She's perfect, from her full, heavy breasts to the flare of her hips and the softness of her belly. I want to worship every inch of her until she understands just how exquisite she is.

"You're so fucking beautiful," I tell her reverently, skimming my hands up her sides. "I could look at you forever and never get tired of it."

Ava flushes under my heated gaze, a delicate pink blooming across her skin. She crosses her arms over her chest self-consciously, as if trying to hide from me.

"Don't," I command gently, taking her wrists and urging her arms back to her sides. "Don't hide from me. I want to see you, all of you."

She bites her lip but nods, allowing me to drink in the sight of her nearly nude body. My hands itch to explore, to map out every curve and valley, to commit her to memory with my touch.

I start at her shoulders, trailing my fingertips down her arms, feeling goosebumps rise in my wake. When I reach her hands, I lace our fingers together, squeezing gently.

"I'm going to make you feel so good, baby," I promise, my voice a husky rasp. "I'm going to touch you until you're trembling, until you're begging for more."

Ava whimpers, her head falling back as I lower my mouth to her neck again. I can't resist tasting her, dragging my tongue over her racing pulse before sucking lightly. She gasps, her fingers tightening around mine.

Releasing one of her hands, I skim my palm down her side, over the dip of her waist and the flare of her hip. Her skin is like satin, impossibly soft and smooth. I want to feel it against me with no barriers between us.

Hooking my fingers in the waistband of her panties, I glance up at her, silently asking for permission. Ava nods, her eyes dark with longing. Slowly, torturously, I drag the scrap of lace down her legs until she can step out of it.

And then she's bare before me. Completely exposed. Mine for the taking.

I have to clench my fists to keep from pouncing on her. She deserves to be savored, worshipped. And I intend to do just that.

Starting at her ankles, I run my hands up her calves, over her knees, along her plush thighs. Ava's breathing grows labored as I near the apex of her thighs, her arousal evident in the slickness coating her folds.

"Ryan," she pants, her hips canting forward. Seeking. Needing.

"I've got you," I assure her. "I'm going to take care of you."

With that vow, I part her glistening lips, groaning at the feel of her molten heat. She's so wet, practically dripping for me. I circle her clit with my thumb, reveling in the choked cry that tears from her throat.

"That's it, let me hear you," I encourage, increasing the pressure on her sensitive bud. "I want to hear every sound you make as I pleasure you."

Ava mewls, her hips bucking against my hand as I tease her entrance with my fingers. She's so tight, her body resisting the intrusion even as she tries to draw me deeper.

"Please," she begs, desperation lacing her tone. "I need...I need..."

"What do you need, baby? Tell me." I dip one finger inside her, just to the first knuckle, marveling at the way her inner muscles clench around me.

"More," Ava gasps. "I need more of you. All of you."

Satisfaction rumbles through me at her plea. Slowly, I ease my finger all the way inside her, groaning at the exquisite feel of her silken walls. She takes me to the hilt, her body welcoming me like I was made for her.

"Oh God," she whimpers, her nails digging into my shoulders. "Ryan..."

"That's it, take my finger. You're doing so well." I pump into her leisurely, letting her grow accustomed to the stretch before adding a second finger.

Ava tenses for a moment, a flicker of discomfort crossing her face before it melts into pure bliss. I scissor my fingers, gently stretching her, preparing her for what's to come.

All the while, I keep up the relentless pressure on her clit, circling and rubbing until she's writhing against me, lost to the pleasure I'm giving her. Her breathy moans and sighs are the sweetest music, urging me to drive her higher.

"I'm...I'm close," she pants, her hips moving frantically now. "Ryan, please...I need..."

"I know what you need." Curling my fingers, I find that spongy spot inside her, massaging ruthlessly. At the same time, I capture her nipple in my mouth, sucking hard as I flick the tip with my tongue.

Ava shrieks, her body going bowstring taut as her orgasm crashes over her. I feel her clenching around my fingers, a flood of wetness coating my hand as she comes apart for me.

I work her through it, easing my touch as the aftershocks roll through her. She collapses against me, her face buried in my neck as she struggles to catch her breath.

"That was...I've never..." She trails off, seeming at a loss for words.

I chuckle, pressing a kiss to her damp temple. "And we're just getting started, sweet girl."

Ava shivers at the promise in my words. When she pulls back to meet my gaze, her eyes are glassy with sated desire, but there's a fledgling hunger there too. She wants more, craves it.

And heaven knows I do too, but just then, we hear the tinkle of her shop bell ring.

Ava freezes and then scrambles to get dressed.

I'm inwardly cursing, my cock aching, yet strangely enough, I'm also sated. Just seeing her fall apart for me was more than enough for me.

She tries to smooth out her ruffled, just-had-her-first-orgasm hair before she hurries to the front of the store with a smile plastered on her face to greet the customer.

I readjust my aching cock and take my leave, but not before I shoot Ava a smoldering look that lets her know I'll be back, and very soon.

Ava Dawson is now *mine*.

four

. . .

Ava

THE BELL above the door jingles and I glance up from the shelves I'm restocking to see Ryan striding into my bookshop. Memories of his fingers buried inside me yesterday send a hot flush across my skin.

"Close up, Ava. I'm taking you to dinner," he commands, his deep voice brooking no argument.

My mouth goes dry. I swallow hard and nod, not trusting myself to speak. As I hurry to flip the sign to "Closed" and lock the front door, I'm acutely aware of Ryan's intense gaze following my every move. The air crackles with unspoken tension.

I grab my purse from behind the counter, my fingers fumbling nervously with the strap. When I turn around, Ryan is right there, crowding into my space. The spicy scent of his cologne invades my senses.

"Ready?" he asks, one eyebrow quirked.

"Y-yes," I stammer, pulse racing as memories of our forbidden tryst replay in my mind—his rough hands gripping my hips, his hardness pressing against me...

I shake my head to clear the scandalous thoughts. Ryan takes my elbow and guides me out the back, his touch searing through my cardigan. I pray he can't feel me trembling as we walk to his car. What is happening to me? I'm not this wanton woman who lets a near stranger take such liberties. And yet, I cannot resist his pull, consequences be damned.

The door shuts with a note of finality and Ryan puts the car in gear. I chance a glance at his chiseled profile.

He doesn't speak as he drives us, and I'm so nervous I can't speak either.

So we sit in a charged silence under we get to our destination.

The restaurant Ryan chooses is dimly lit and intimate. Surprisingly, it's one I've never been to, and I've been almost everywhere here.

We're sitting secluded in a back booth, knees brushing beneath the table, and the rest of the world falls away. I fidget with my water glass, hyperaware of his closeness.

"So tell me about yourself, Ava," Ryan prompts, his deep baritone sending shivers down my spine. "What's a beautiful woman like you doing all alone in this small town?"

I lift one shoulder in a shrug, trying to appear casual despite my racing heart. "I've always lived here. The bookshop was my grandmother's—it's my life now. My safe haven." Until he upended everything.

"Hmm." His blue eyes study me intently, seeing too much.

I flush at his heated gaze. "What about you? You never did tell me what you do." I boldly meet his gaze. Two can play at this game.

Ryan's jaw clenches and he looks away. "I'm a cop from the city. I'm on mandatory leave. There was...an incident. A suspect...I broke protocol. The slimeball hit a woman, so I shot him. He didn't die, but I was supposed to just arrest him—not seek vigilante justice." He scoffs, "They thought I should take some time away to clear my head."

My heart clenches and melts at the same time.

He was trying to protect a woman, and it might have cost him his job. Impulsively, I reach across the table and lay my hand over his. "I'm so sorry, Ryan. That must be really hard."

His hand turns beneath mine, fingers intertwining. The pad of his thumb strokes across my sensitive skin and I barely suppress a gasp. Electric currents zing through my body at the simple touch.

"Ava." His eyes blaze into mine, dark with emotion and something more feral.

Desire.

Possession.

The intensity steals my breath. This connection between us...it defies reason. I should run far away from this man and the dangerous feelings he evokes. But I'm caught in his orbit, a satellite helpless to resist his gravitational pull.

Abruptly, Ryan signals for the check, tossing bills on the table. "Let's get out of here." His tone brooks no argument.

Pulse pounding, I follow him out into the night.

The short drive back to the bookshop passes in a blur, the cool night air doing nothing to douse the heat simmering under my skin. Ryan's hand rests possessively on my thigh, branding me through the thin fabric of my dress.

We barely make it through the door before he's

on me, crowding me back against the nearest bookshelf. Novels topple to the floor unheeded as his solid frame presses into my softer curves, igniting flames of desire that lick through my veins.

"I've wanted to do this all night," he rasps, breath hot against my neck. "You're driving me crazy, Ava."

"Ryan..." His name escapes on a breathy moan as his lips blaze a trail along my jaw. Large hands grip my hips, fingers digging deliciously into my flesh.

I'm drowning in sensation, my mind clouding with lust. I know I should stop this, put some distance between us. But my body betrays me, arching into his touch, silently begging for more.

Cool air kisses my heated skin as he drags down the zipper of my dress. It pools at my feet and I shiver, from the chill and the molten look in Ryan's eyes as he takes me in. Like a wolf sizing up his prey.

"Beautiful," he breathes reverently, callused palms gliding over my sides to cup my heavy breasts. I gasp as he rolls the hardened peaks between his fingers, sparks of pleasured pain shooting straight to my core.

"Please..." I whimper, not even knowing what

I'm asking for. I just need him to quench this inferno he's stoked to life inside me.

Fisting a hand in my hair, Ryan tilts my head back and crashes his mouth over mine in a commanding kiss. It's hot, wet, and filthy—a brutish claiming that steals the air from my lungs and the strength from my knees.

His tongue delves deep, stroking over mine in blatant imitation of the carnal act our bodies crave. He tastes of whiskey and sin and broken promises, an addictive flavor I know I'll never get enough of.

Kissing Ryan is a revelation, the rest of the world fading away until there is only this—his hard body aligned with mine, the scrape of his stubble against my tingling lips, the wicked thrust of his tongue that sends bolts of lust sizzling down my spine.

I'm lost to the drugging passion, my fingers fisting in the fabric of his shirt as I pull him impossibly closer, wanting to crawl inside his skin. My thighs part in wanton invitation, the damp lace of my panties an undeniable testament to my arousal.

Ryan takes ruthless advantage, notching a powerful thigh between mine, the thick muscle pressing right where I'm throbbing and aching for his touch. Unbidden, my hips rock against him, seeking a firmer pressure, silently begging him to sate the clawing need building in my core.

He tears his mouth from mine with a harsh groan, the sound reverberating through the air between us. "Fuck, Ava. You're killing me."

His voice is little more than a growl, eyes blazing down at me with an intensity that steals my breath. I've never seen a man like this—on the verge of losing ironclad control because of *me*.

There's a predatory edge to his gaze that should terrify me but only makes me burn hotter, an answering wildness rising up from someplace hidden deep inside.

I want him to unleash it. Devour me. Brand his mark on my skin for all the world to see. Consequences no longer matter—only assuaging this fever pitch need that threatens to consume me.

Blindly, I reach between us, hands shaking slightly as I attack the fastenings of his jeans. Just as I get the button free, tugging on the zipper, a sudden noise from outside shatters the lust-soaked haze enveloping us.

We jerk apart, panting harshly, staring at each other with passion-glazed eyes as the reality of what almost happened crashes down like a bucket of ice water. Common sense filters back in, dousing the flames.

Ryan scrubs a hand over his face, muttering something under his breath. "I should go check that out, make sure everything's safe."

The words are like a knife to my heart but I nod anyway, knowing it's for the best. If he stayed, we'd wind up naked and sweaty, with him buried to the hilt inside me. And then everything would change in ways I don't think either of us is ready for.

Disappointment and frustration carve hollow aches in my chest as he zips up and steps back, putting necessary space between us before the tenuous hold on our control snaps again.

"I'll be right back, Ava," he rumbles as he turns away, the set of his broad shoulders tense. Three long strides carry him out the door, the bell tinkling forlornly in his wake.

Leaving me to slump against the bookshelf in a boneless heap, my blood still thrumming with unsated arousal, staring blankly at his retreating back.

When he comes back, I feign a headache and apologetically bid him goodnight.

The look on his face tells me he's not buying it for a minute, but he doesn't press me.

I'm both disappointed and relieved.

———

Sleep is a long time coming that night, my body restless and wound tight. I toss and turn until the wee hours, replaying every moment of that searing kiss. The feel of Ryan's hands on my skin, the taste of his lips, the delicious heat and hardness pressing me into the bookshelf...

It haunts my fevered dreams, tormenting me with pleasure just out of reach. I wake gasping his name, my heart aching and my thighs clenched together to ease the incessant throbbing at their apex.

Damn him. Damn my traitorous body. Damn this inexplicable connection drawing us together against all rhyme and reason.

I drag myself through my morning routine in a daze, exhaustion and frustration warring for dominance as I open up the shop and go through the motions. But even as I try to focus on alphabetizing new arrivals, my mind drifts constantly back to him.

Ryan Callahan has turned my quiet, ordinary life upside down and inside out in the space of days. And I have a sinking suspicion he's only just getting started.

God help me, but I'm not sure I have the strength to resist. Or if I even want to anymore.

The day limps by in agonizing slowness. I

startle at every creak and groan of the old building, half-expecting him to appear around every corner. But as the hours tick by, it becomes painfully clear that our heated encounter was nothing more than a momentary distraction for him.

Biting back my disappointment, I remind myself that it's for the best. I've always been better off alone anyway, living vicariously through the pages of my beloved novels. Safe from heartache and betrayal.

———

Ryan

I'm a damned fool, leaving her there like that. Wound up and wanting, same as me. What the hell was I thinking?

I wasn't. That's the problem. One taste of sweet Ava and my brain short-circuits, overridden by sheer animal lust. I've never lost control so fast, not even as a horny teenager.

I should have pushed her. She wouldn't have resisted me. I'd have her in my arms right now.

I've never been so turned inside out over a woman. There's something about Ava.

I know she's it for me. This woman is all I'm going to want for the rest of my life. The possessiveness I feel every time I think of her is more intense than any instinct I've ever had.

Pacing my rented cabin, I scrub a hand over my face and groan. I should be reviewing case files, trying to find a way to fight back against the case that got me benched. Instead all I can think about is lush curves, trembling sighs, slick heat clenching around my fingers as she shattered...

Fuck. At this rate, I'll be waking up to sticky sheets like some pimply adolescent. A cold shower and a few miles on the treadmill do nothing to drive Ava from my thoughts. Her scent clings to my skin, honeyed musk and old books.

She's an addiction already and I've barely touched her. Innocent and untouched, yet responding so eagerly, greedily taking what I gave her. Begging for more with those big green eyes when I withdrew.

Christ, I'm in trouble. I want to corrupt her, claim her, make her mine in every depraved way imaginable. Tie her to my bed and pleasure that succulent body until she screams.

Sleep is impossible, my cock throbbing

painfully at vivid X-rated visions dancing behind my eyelids. Of Ava on her knees, looking up at me as she takes me into her mouth. Spread eagle, flushed and panting as I feast on her pretty pink pussy. Riding me hard and fast, tits bouncing, head thrown back in ecstasy...

I fist myself with rough, furious strokes, grunting as I spill over my hand, her name a reverent curse on my lips. But climax brings no relief, no lessening of the clawing need.

I'm going to have her. Consequences be damned. Ava Dawson is *mine*.

five

. . .

Ryan

I'M HIKING in the mountains because they're supposed to bring clarity or some bullshit.

But all I think about is Ava and how she's been avoiding me. When I show up at the bookshop, she quickly gets on the phone or finds a customer to help.

And I'm going fucking nuts. All I can think of is her.

Even now as I trek through the winding trails, my mind wanders back to her, to the softness of her curves, the depths of her soulful eyes.

I *need* to see her, need to feel her presence like I

need my next breath. Before I can second guess myself, I pull out my phone and dial the number for her bookstore. It might be a dirty trick, but a man's got to do what a man's got to do.

She answers on the second ring.

"Ava," I breathe her name like a prayer, my voice coming out rough and gravelly.

"Ryan?" Her voice is breathy, surprised. "Um, how can I help you?"

"I just..." I pause, searching for the right words. "I'm going for a hike, up in the mountains. I was wondering if you'd like to join me?"

Silence stretches between us, filled with unspoken longing and hesitation. I hold my breath, waiting.

"I...I don't know, Ryan. I have the store and..."

"Just for a few hours. Please, Ava. I need...I just need some company." *You. I need you.*

She sighs softly, and I can picture her worrying her bottom lip. "Okay. Okay, I'll come."

Relief floods through me, followed by a surge of anticipation. "Great. I'll pick you up in an hour."

As I hang up, my heart pounds in my chest. An hour. One hour until I have her all to myself, away from prying eyes and interruptions.

The drive to Ava's is a blur, my mind consumed with thoughts of her. When I pull up outside her store, she's already waiting, dressed in form-fitting hiking gear that hugs her luscious curves. I swallow hard, my body tightening with need.

"Ready?" I ask as she climbs into the passenger seat.

She nods, her eyes meeting mine briefly before darting away. The air between us crackles with tension, the confined space of the car amplifying every breath, every shift.

The winding road takes us higher, the town disappearing in the rearview mirror. With each mile, the anticipation builds, coiling tighter and tighter within me. Ava stares out the window, her hands twisting in her lap. I long to reach over, to still her nervous movements and lace my fingers with hers.

Finally, we arrive at the trailhead, the mountain looming before us. We set off in silence, the only sounds the crunch of our footsteps and the distant calls of birds. The trail is narrow, forcing us to walk single file. I let Ava take the lead, my eyes drawn to the sway of her hips, the flex of her calves.

The higher we climb, the more the rest of the world falls away. Up here, it's just us, two souls drawn together by an inexplicable force. The air grows thinner, and Ava's breathing becomes more labored. I place my hand on the small of her back, feeling the heat of her skin through her thin shirt.

"You okay?" I murmur, my lips close to her ear.

She nods, leaning into my touch for a brief moment before continuing on. Every brush of our bodies, every shared glance, is amplified in the seclusion of the mountains. The connection between us grows stronger with each step, the desire more urgent.

I need to touch her, to feel her soft skin under my fingertips. I need to taste her, to claim her as mine. The primal urge rises within me, threatening to overtake my control.

But I hold back, letting the anticipation build, knowing that when we finally come together, it will be explosive. The mountains will bear witness to our passion, to the inevitable collision of our bodies and souls.

For now, I content myself with the knowledge that she's here, with me, away from the world's prying eyes. In the solitude of nature, anything can happen. And I intend to make sure it does.

———

We crest the peak and we're met with a breathtaking view. The sun dips below the horizon, casting the sky ablaze with hues of red and gold. But the real beauty, the true prize, stands before me. Ava's cheeks are flushed, her eyes shining with a mix of wonder and something else, something I can only hope is desire.

I can't take it anymore. I need her. *Now.*

My hand shakes as I cup her delicate chin, gently tilting her head back. Her breath catches in her throat, and her eyes darken with longing.

"Ryan," she whispers, her voice a siren's call that lures me in.

"Ava," I growl, my voice low and dangerous. "I want you, Ava. More than I've ever wanted anything."

Her eyes widen, but she doesn't pull away. Instead, she leans in, her plump lips a mere breath away from mine. My heart hammers in my chest, and my cock throbs in anticipation.

"Ryan," she breathes, her voice like velvet.

And that…the sound of my name on her lips, all breathy like that is the last straw. The final barrier shatters, and I claim her mouth in a searing kiss, my tongue delving into her heat, tasting her sweetness. Ava moans into my mouth, her fingers tangling in my hair, and any semblance of restraint I have left evaporates.

I tear my mouth from hers, trailing scorching

kisses down her jaw, along her neck, to the valley between her breasts. Her soft, curvy body trembles beneath me, and I relish in the knowledge that it's me she's whimpering for.

Me who's going to be balls deep inside her.

Me who's going to claim her.

With a groan, I yank her shirt upwards, revealing her luscious, full breasts spilling out of her bra. Her nipples are hard, aflame against her silky skin, and I can't help but moan at the sight. Ava arches her back, pressing her chest closer to my face.

I lift her leg to my hip and back her against a tree. I trail my tongue down her cleavage, teasing one sensitive nipple as my hands fumble with her jeans. I can't get them off fast enough.

Finally, her jeans pool around her ankles, revealing her matching, lacy panties, drenched with her arousal. Ava's cheeks flush a delicious shade of pink, but she doesn't try to hide herself from me. Instead, she bites her lip, a look of wanton desire in her eyes.

"You're so beautiful," I murmur, before I sweep my tongue across her heated slit, eliciting a gasp from her.

Ava's hands twist in my hair as I feast on her,

teasing her swollen folds, drinking her in like I've been thirsty my entire life. She tastes like ambrosia.

I can't take it anymore, and I pull my cock from my pants. The way Ava's eyes widen as she takes in my swollen length only serves to heighten my arousal.

I hold her eyes as I jack off. I don't mean to go all the way, but before I can control myself, I feel my cum shooting up my stalk.

I grab Ava's shirt and pull it up as I aim myself at her stomach. I groan as white, sticky ropes pulse from my swollen head, landing on Ava's soft skin and trickling down to her belly button.

Ava gasps as my hot seed splatters across her smooth stomach. Her eyes are wide with surprise and dark with desire as she watches me mark her creamy skin.

"Ryan," she breathes, her voice dripping with need. "I...I want..."

I capture her lips in a searing kiss before she can finish her sentence. I already know what she wants, what she needs. It's the same primal hunger coursing through my veins.

With a low growl, I lift her up, encouraging her legs to wrap around my waist. The head of my still-hard cock nudges against her soaked entrance and we both moan at the contact. Slowly, inch by delicious inch, I sink into her tight, wet heat.

"Fuck, Ava," I groan against the shell of her ear. "You feel so good wrapped around my cock."

She whimpers and arches against me, silently begging for more. I give her what she craves, thrusting into her with deep, powerful strokes. The rough bark of the tree scrapes against her back but she doesn't seem to care, lost in the throes of passion.

"Harder," she pants, her nails digging into my shoulders. "Please Ryan, fuck me harder."

I comply with a savage snarl, pistoning my hips and driving into her sopping cunt with wild abandon. Her needy cries echo through the tranquil forest as I take her, claim her, make her mine.

My balls tighten and I know I'm close. Reaching between our sweat-slicked bodies, I find her swollen clit, rubbing tight circles around the sensitive nub. Ava thrashes in my arms, her pussy clenching around my shaft as her orgasm crashes over her.

"That's it, baby," I coax her, never letting up. "Come for me. Come all over my fucking cock."

With a keening moan, she shatters, her silken walls fluttering and milking my dick. I thrust once, twice more before burying myself to the hilt and emptying my seed deep inside her trembling body.

For a long moment, we stay locked together, chests heaving, hearts pounding in sync. Ava buries her face in the crook of my neck, her lips brushing my sweat-dampened skin. I press a tender kiss to her temple, savoring the feel of her, the scent of her.

"You're mine now, Ava," I rasp, still buried inside her. "There's no going back. Not after this."

She lifts her head, her eyes meeting mine. In their depths, I see everything I feel reflected back at me—the desire, the need, the unbreakable connection.

"I'm yours, Ryan," she whispers, her voice thick with emotion. "I always have been."

As the sun dips below the horizon, painting the sky in vibrant oranges and pinks, we reluctantly disentangle our bodies. Ava's cheeks are flushed, her hair mussed from our passionate encounter. She looks thoroughly debauched and utterly gorgeous.

I help her back into her clothes, my hands lingering on her soft curves. I can't resist stealing another kiss, savoring the taste of her, the feel of her pliant body against mine.

She's *mine.*

six

. . .

Ava

I **FEEL** the warmth of Ryan's body fading as I slip out of the vehicle, the chill of uncertainty seeping into my skin. The afterglow of our passionate encounter dims under the weight of reality—he's only here temporarily, bound to return to his life in the city.

My pulse races as I scramble to grab my purse. I can't let myself get swept up in a fantasy, no matter how much my body aches for his touch, how much my heart yearns to surrender. I have to protect myself.

Ryan reaches across the console, his hand reaching for me. "Ava? What's wrong?"

I force a smile, but it feels brittle. "Nothing. I just...I have to get back to the bookstore." The lie tastes bitter on my tongue.

He sits up straighter, alert. His eyes search mine, perceptive and piercing. "Did I do something?"

"No, no...it's not you." My voice wavers. I avert my gaze, focusing on buttoning my blouse with trembling fingers.

Ryan moves closer, his warmth enveloping me again. "Talk to me, Ava. I can tell something's bothering you."

I inhale sharply, his scent flooding my senses—a heady mix of musk and desire that makes my knees weak. I steel myself against the magnetic pull, the urge to fall back into his arms and forget the inevitable heartache.

"I'm fine, Ryan. Really. I just need some space." The words feel jagged in my throat.

His brow furrows, confusion and concern etched in the lines of his handsome face. "Space? Did I come on too strong? I thought..." He trails off, uncertainty clouding his eyes.

I shake my head, a lump forming in my throat.

How can I explain the war raging inside me? The battle between yearning and self-preservation?

"It's not that. I just...I can't do this." My voice breaks on the last word.

Ryan reaches for my hand, his touch searing my skin. "Can't do what? Ava, please, help me understand."

I pull away, wrapping my arms around myself as if I could shield my heart from the impending pain. "This...us...whatever this is. It's temporary, Ryan. You're going to leave, and I'll be..."

The unspoken word hangs heavy in the air between us. *Alone. Abandoned.* Just like always.

Ryan's eyes widen, realization dawning. He gets out of the Jeep and makes his way around the front to me.

"Ava..." He takes a step towards me, but I back away, my resolve crumbling with each passing second.

"I have to go." I finally grab my purse, my vision blurring with unshed tears. "I'm sorry."

Before he can respond, I flee, my heart shattering with every step. The door closes behind me with a resounding finality, sealing in the memory of his touch, his taste, his love.

A love I'm terrified to claim as my own.

seven

. . .

Ava

I STRUGGLE to focus on the books I'm shelving, my mind still reeling from last night's abrupt departure. Ryan's face, etched with confusion and concern, haunts me. The chime of the door startles me, and I turn to find him standing there, his presence filling the small bookstore.

"Ava, we need to talk." His voice is gentle but firm, his eyes searching mine for answers.

I swallow hard, my grip tightening on the book in my hand. "There's nothing to talk about, Ryan. I told you, this...it's not going to work."

He steps closer, his warmth enveloping me. "Why? Because you think I'm going to leave? Ava, I'm not going anywhere."

I laugh bitterly, the sound hollow in my ears. "That's what they all say. But in the end, they always leave. And I'm left picking up the pieces of my shattered heart."

His eyes darken. "Who's they?"

I swallow. "My ex, and…and my dad." Admitting the truth hurts. That my dad ran out on me after my mom dad, leaving me all alone with my grandma—who was wonderful, but still. It hurts that I wasn't enough. That he left.

Ryan's hand cups my cheek, his thumb brushing away a stray tear I didn't even realize had fallen. "I'm not like them, Ava. I would never hurt you."

I shake my head, pulling away from his touch. "You can't promise that. No one can."

I turn away, busying myself with straightening the already immaculate shelves.

His hand on my shoulder gently turns me back to face him. "Ava, listen to me. I know what it's like to be afraid of getting hurt. I've been there."

I meet his gaze, surprised by the raw vulnerability I see there. "What do you mean?"

He takes a deep breath, as if steeling himself. "My mom left when I was a kid. Just packed up and walked out one day, no explanation. And my dad...he wasn't exactly the nurturing type. I grew up thinking that love was a weakness, that it only led to pain."

My heart aches for the little boy he once was, the man he's become despite it all. "Ryan, I'm so sorry."

He shakes his head, a sad smile on his lips. "I'm not telling you this for sympathy, Ava. I'm telling you because I want you to understand that I get it. I know how hard it is to trust, to let someone in. But I also know that if you don't take that risk, you'll miss out on something incredible."

I bite my lip, torn between the desire to fall into his arms and the fear of what will happen when he inevitably leaves.

His fingers trail up my spine, igniting sparks beneath my skin. I shiver, pressing closer, needing to feel every inch of him against me.

"Ava," he breathes, his lips brushing my ear. "You're so fucking beautiful."

I tilt my head back, meeting his heated gaze. "I'm not-"

"Don't." His grip tightens, his eyes intense.

"Don't put yourself down. You are gorgeous, inside and out. And I'm going to spend every damn day proving it to you until you believe it."

Tears prick my eyes at the fervor in his words. No one has ever made me feel so seen, so cherished. "Ryan..."

"I mean it, sweetheart. I'm here, and I'm not going anywhere. Not unless you tell me to."

I shake my head vehemently. "No. Stay. Please."

A slow smile spreads across his face, his dimple appearing. "There's nowhere else I'd rather be."

Then his mouth is on mine, hot and demanding. I moan into the kiss, parting my lips to grant him access. His tongue sweeps inside, claiming me, consuming me.

I lose myself in the sensations—the rasp of his stubble against my skin, the press of his hard body, the intoxicating taste of him. All the doubts and insecurities fade away until there's nothing but this moment, this man.

His hands roam my curves, leaving trails of fire in their wake. I arch into his touch, silently begging for more. He growls in approval, his fingers slipping beneath the hem of my sweater to splay across my bare skin.

"Ryan, please..." I'm not even sure what I'm asking for, I just know I need him like I need air.

"I've got you, baby," he promises, his voice raw with desire. "I'll give you everything."

And as he carries me upstairs and lowers me onto the bed, his weight deliciously heavy, I believe him.

Ryan's hands skim along my ribcage, his touch electric even through the fabric of my top. I shiver, my skin pebbling with goosebumps as anticipation builds low in my belly.

His fingers dip beneath the hem, brushing against the sensitive skin there. I suck in a sharp breath. He pauses, his eyes seeking permission.

I nod, not trusting my voice. Slowly, reverently, he lifts the garment up and over my head, tossing it aside. Cool air washes over my exposed skin but it's quickly chased away by the heat of his gaze.

"So fucking beautiful," he murmurs, almost to himself.

Self-consciousness battles with desire as his eyes rake over me slowly. I know he's seen me before, but this time is different. It's slow and purposeful and…vulnerable. I fight the urge to cover myself, to hide the soft curves and stretch marks that map my body's history.

As if sensing my unease, Ryan leans down, trailing gentle kisses along my collarbone, up the column of my throat. "Perfect," he whispers against my pulse point. "Every inch of you."

Tears prick behind my eyelids at the raw sincerity in his tone. I run my fingers through his hair, anchoring him to me. He lavishes attention on my neck, my jaw, painting devotion with his lips and tongue.

My hands slip beneath his shirt, eager to map the hard planes of his back, the flex of muscle. He helps me strip it off before lowering his bulk onto me again, skin against skin.

The rough dusting of his chest hair abrading my nipples sends sparks of pleasure through me. I hook a leg over his hip, drawing him closer, savoring the weight of him.

Our mouths meet again, deep and drugging. There's no rush despite the intensity, just a slow, thorough exploration. He tastes like coming home and new beginnings all at once.

I lose myself to sensation—touch and taste and scent. The rest of the world falls away until there is only us, only this. Two broken souls finding solace in each other.

His hands are everywhere—cupping my breasts, tracing my curves, sending shivers down my spine. Mine are just as greedy, learning every inch of him.

When his fingers slip between my thighs, I gasp aloud. The sensation of being touched there sends my mind reeling. Ryan teases me expertly, nudging at my entrance before swirling back up to stroke my clit.

The pleasure spikes, white-hot and blinding. "Ryan," I pant.

"I've got you, baby," he growls, and then his mouth is on me, sucking my clit into his mouth, tongue flicking and lapping until I'm sobbing his name and flying apart.

The orgasm rocks me to my core, leaving me breathless and shaking in its wake.

Ryan's not done with me yet. He hoists himself over me, brushing the hair from my face. "Look at me," he demands, his eyes blazing.

I meet his gaze, drowning in the intensity I find there. "Yours," I gasp.

A smile tugs at his lips, a wicked glint in his eye. "That's right, Ava. You're mine."

Then he's inside me, hard and deep, stretching me in the best possible way. I tighten around him, my body reacting to his on instinct.

He thrusts—slow at first, then picking up speed. Each powerful stroke sets me on fire.

"Tell me you want me," he commands.

"I...I want you, Ryan," I moan, my cheeks

flushing but my need overpowering any lingering shyness.

He growls in response, burying his face in the crook of my neck as he thrusts deeper, harder. "Say it louder, baby. Beg for me."

"I want you, Ryan! I need you!" The words tumble out of my mouth, unfiltered and raw, and God, it feels good.

His response is wordless, a groan torn from his throat as he picks up the pace. I can feel the tension coiling tighter and tighter, the heat between my legs building once more.

"That's it," he grunts, "come for me again, Ava. Come with me."

The world tilts on its axis as I do just that, spiraling over the edge with an almighty cry. Ryan follows, his body tensing above mine before collapsing against me, breathing ragged, spent.

As we catch our breath, our hearts pounding in tandem, I look into his eyes and see a truth there that I've never seen before.

"I...I love you, Ava," he whispers between breaths, his eyes brimming with emotion.

Tears well up in my own as I stroke his cheek tenderly. "I love you too, Ryan."

We stay entwined for what feels like an eternity, our bodies still joined as our pulses gradually slow to a normal rhythm. The room around us fades away, and it's like it's just the two of us in this world.

"I'm never going to fucking leave you, you beautiful thing. You're mine."

eight

. . .

Ryan

MY PHONE BUZZES INCESSANTLY in my pocket as Ava and I walk hand in hand through the quiet streets. I ignore it at first, not wanting anything to interrupt this perfect moment with her. But the vibrations persist urgently.

"Sorry, I should probably check this," I mutter, flashing Ava an apologetic look. She nods understandingly as I reluctantly pull out my phone.

"Callahan." I bark into the receiver. It's my Captain from the precinct. There's been a major break in the Carmichael case and they need all hands on deck. I'm being called back to the city immediately.

"I understand," I reply curtly before hanging up. A heavy sigh escapes my lips as I turn to face Ava. Her brows are knitted together in concern, those soulful eyes searching mine.

"What is it? What's wrong?" She asks softly, squeezing my hand.

"That was work. There's an emergency and they need me back in the city ASAP." I explain, my jaw clenching in frustration.

Her face falls and she pulls her hand away, folding her arms protectively across her chest. "Oh. I see." She replies, her voice tinged with resignation. "Well, I suppose this mountain town fantasy couldn't last forever..."

I reach for her, but she takes a step back. "Ava, wait, it's not like that. This thing between us, it's real."

But I can see the doubts taking root behind her eyes, the way her shoulders hunch inward. "It's fine, Ryan. I get it. You have your big city life to get back to. And I have my little bookstore. We're from different worlds."

"That's not true! Ava, please. Just let me explain —" But she's already turning away from me, picking up her pace.

"I should go. Safe travels back to the city, Officer Callahan." She says over her shoulder, her voice cracking on my name.

I watch helplessly as she retreats down the sidewalk, her curvy figure disappearing around the corner. Fuck! I scrub a hand over my face.

What Ava and I have is special. In just a short time, she's turned my world upside down in the best way. Those soft curves, that brilliant mind, the way she looks at me like I'm her hero...I can't lose her.

I start moving in the direction she went, determined to make this right. To make Ava understand that no distance can change how I feel about her. That this small town girl has completely captured my big city heart.

My heart pounds as I pick up the pace. The city can wait—I have to find Ava now. I sprint in the direction she ran off, scanning the quaint storefronts lining the street.

Then I hear it—a scream piercing the air up ahead.

Ava.

Rounding the corner, I see red. Some scumbag has his filthy hand clamped around Ava's arm as she struggles to break free, her beautiful face etched with fear.

"Get your fucking hands off her!" I roar, closing the distance in a fury. The adrenaline is singing in my veins.

The guy looks up, startled, his grip loosening just enough for Ava to wrench herself away. She stumbles back, clutching her arm. My vision tunnels on the soon-to-be dead man.

"Who the hell are you?" He spits, squaring up to me. I can tell by his weaselly face this is Ava's dirtbag ex. Call me a stalker, but I quickly put all my cop resources to work and found out just how the fucker was when I found out about him. The one who made her doubt herself, broke her heart.

I don't bother with a response. I let my fists do the talking. One solid crack to his jaw sends him reeling. He swings wildly but I dodge, my training kicking in, and land another blow to his gut. He doubles over with a wheeze.

Grabbing his collar, I wrench him up to snarl in his face.

"I hear you're a city boy. If you know what's best for you, you'll crawl back into whatever gutter you crawled out of. Got it? And if you ever so much as look at her again, I will end you. Understand?"

He makes a choking sound I take for assent.

With a final shove, he crumples into a pile on the pavement, out cold.

Breath heaving, I turn to Ava. She's staring at her ex's prone form, then up at me, her green eyes wide and glassy with shock.

"Ryan..." she whispers, starting to tremble.

In two strides I'm there, pulling her tight against my chest. She clings to me, hands fisting in my shirt.

"I've got you, sweetheart," I murmur into her hair, running soothing hands down her back. "You're safe. I'm here."

I'll always be here for her, no matter what. This brave, beautiful woman has me, body and soul. And somehow, I'm going to prove it to her.

I hoist her up in my arms, ignoring her startled squeak. "What?" I grin down at her. "Am I not the strong, rugged hero you dreamed of?"

Ava blushes.

That blush does wonders for my ego. I carry her back to her store, up the stairs to her cozy apartment above. Kicking the door shut, I lower her to her feet.

"Stay," I growl, voice gravelly with need as I unbutton my shirt.

Her eyes devour every inch of bared skin, sending a red-hot pulse straight to my groin.

I push my pants down, freeing my rock-hard erection. Her eyes widen, then travel down my form.

"Ryan..." she whimpers, desire glazing her eyes.

"Tell me what you want, kitten."

"You," she moans, uncrossing her arms to tug at her hoodie. "I want you, Ryan. So badly."

"Damn right, you do." I stalk towards her, backing her against the wall. "And you're gonna have all of me, Ava. Every inch, until you're branded with my touch."

I crush my lips to hers, devouring her sweetness. Ava responds with equal fervor, her soft curves molding against me seamlessly.

"Do you not get how obsessed with you I am?" I manage between kisses, trailing my lips down her neck. "All these beautiful curves are *mine*."

Her breath hitches as I cup her breast, thumbing her hard nipple through her shirt. "Ryan..."

"Say it, Ava. Tell me who you belong to."

"Y-you," she gasps, hips arching into my touch.

"I'll fuck you so hard, I'll put a baby in you," I growl, slipping a hand between her legs, finding her drenched. "So the entire world will know who you belong to."

"Yes, yes, please."

Those words are my undoing. I pick her up,

slamming her against the wall. Her legs wrap around my waist.

"Ryan," she moans, digging her nails into my shoulders.

"I got you, kitten." I slip inside her, filling her to the hilt. "So fucking tight."

"Ryan!" she screams, her head thrown back.

I start a punishing pace, thrusting into her, claiming every inch that's rightfully mine. Ava's nails rake my back as she moans my name endlessly. This complex, curvy goddess is my undoing.

"You feel so good, Ava," I groan, picking up the pace. "So damn good."

"Ryan, I..."

"What, kitten?" I growl, teasing her clit.

"I...love...you," she pants, arching her back. "Please don't ever leave me."

Those three words and her broken plea send me over the edge. With one final thrust, I explode inside her, roaring my release. As my dick convulses, pumping her full of my seed, Ava's body shatters around me, her walls clenching me tighter than ever before.

"I could never leave you, baby. You're mine. Now and forever," I tell her as I brush a strand of hair from her forehead, admiring her flushed face and the glowing sheen of sweat on her brow. Ava's eyes flutter open, hazy with satisfaction and something deeper, more profound.

"You really mean that?" She whispers, vulnerability seeping into her tone. "Even with your big important job back in the city?"

I cup her face tenderly, holding her emerald gaze with the intensity of my conviction. "Ava, listen to me. Yeah, my job is important. But you...you're everything."

I punctuate my declaration with a searing kiss, pouring every ounce of my devotion into the press of my lips against hers. She melts into me, her fingers threading through my hair.

"I love you," I murmur against her mouth. "So damn much. And I'll spend every day proving it to you if that's what it takes."

Ava smiles tremulously, her eyes shining with unshed tears. "I love you too, Ryan. I never thought I could feel this way about someone."

"Believe it, kitten." I flash her a roguish grin. "You're stuck with me now. No take backs."

She laughs, the sweet sound warming me from the inside out. "I suppose there are worse fates."

"Damn straight." I nuzzle her neck, inhaling her intoxicating scent. "In fact, I can think of a few I'd like to explore with you right now..."

Ava shivers as I nip at her sensitive skin. "Again? But what about—"

"The city will still be there tomorrow, and you can bet your ass I'm never going back there without taking you with me. From now on, where I go, you go, and vice versa," I assure her, walking us towards the bed. "Tonight, I plan on worshipping every single inch of you."

I lay her down on the quilt, taking a moment to admire the way her hair fans out on the pillow, her kiss-swollen lips, the heaving of her perfect breasts. My eyes rake over her sumptuous curves possessively.

"God, you're so fucking beautiful," I rasp, my voice thick with renewed desire. "I will never get enough of you."

"Then take me," Ava challenges, a newfound boldness in her eyes as she reaches for me. "I'm yours, Ryan. Completely."

A primal growl rumbles in my chest as I cover her body with mine once more, losing myself in her honeyed lips and velvet heat. This right here, buried inside the woman I love, is the only home I'll ever need.

The rest of the world fades away as we make love, slow and deep, savoring each gasp and moan, every tremor and clutch. With each powerful thrust, I pour my devotion into her willing body, branding myself on her very soul.

Ava arches beneath me, crying out her pleasure into the charged air, her nails scoring my back. I groan her name like a prayer as her silken walls flutter around me.

"That's it, baby. Take all of me," I encourage her through gritted teeth, fighting the urge to explode as her tight heat clenches me like a vice. "You feel how hard you make me? How crazy you drive me?"

"Yes! Oh God, Ryan!" Ava sobs, writhing beneath my pistoning hips. "Don't stop, please don't ever stop!"

"Never," I vow, reaching between us to circle her swollen clit. "I'll never stop loving you, Ava. Fucking you. Filling this sweet pussy with my cum."

She keens high in her throat, back bowing off the bed as her orgasm crashes over her. Her walls spasm around my throbbing cock, milking me for all I'm worth. With a guttural shout, I bury myself to the hilt and let go, painting her womb with thick ropes of my seed.

"Ava!" I roar, hips jerking erratically as I empty myself inside her fluttering channel. Distantly, I'm aware of her fingers digging into my ass, pulling me impossibly deeper.

"Yes, Ryan! Fill me up!" She moans wantonly, grinding herself against me. "I want it all. Want to be dripping with you."

"Fuck!" I hiss, stars exploding behind my eyelids at her filthy words. This shy, sweet book-worm is going to be the death of me. The best kind of death.

Slowly, I collapse on top of her, careful not to crush her. Ava's arms immediately wind around my neck, fingers toying with the sweat-dampened hair at my nape. I nuzzle into the crook of her shoulder, pressing languid kisses to her fevered skin.

"I love you," she whispers, her voice quavering with emotion. "I love you so much it terrifies me."

I lift my head to meet her shimmering gaze, my heart clenching at the vulnerability I find there. Cupping her face, I brush my thumbs over her flushed cheekbones.

"I know, baby. I feel it too. This thing between us...it's big. Life-changing." I drop a tender kiss to her trembling lips. "But I'm not going anywhere, Ava. You're it for me. The endgame."

A radiant smile blooms across her face, so beautiful it steals my breath. She draws me down for another slow, deep kiss that sets my blood on fire all over again.

"Show me," she murmurs against my mouth. "Show me how much you love me, Ryan."

And I do. Over and over, worshipping her body with reverent hands and ardent lips, until the first rays of dawn paint her satiated flesh in strokes of gold.

epilogue

. . .

One year later

Ava

THE BELL above the bookshop door jingles cheerfully as Ryan pushes it open, his strong frame filling the entryway. My heart flutters at the sight of my husband, as it does every day when he arrives for our lunch date.

"Hey beautiful," he greets me, his deep voice sending shivers down my spine. His electric blue eyes rake over my curves appreciatively as he strides over to me.

"Hi handsome," I reply shyly, a blush heating

my cheeks. Even after a year of marriage, Ryan still makes me feel like a giddy schoolgirl with his intense gaze and commanding presence.

And holy fuck, does he look hot in his policeman uniform. Seriously, I never thought I was one of those girls who swooned at men in uniform, but my husband in his uniform is enough to get me dripping wet every time.

He reaches me and pulls me into his strong arms, enveloping me in his warm, musky scent. I melt into his embrace, relishing the feel of his hard body pressed against my soft one. His large hand slides possessively over the curve of my bottom.

"Missed you, baby," he murmurs huskily, nuzzling into my neck and placing a hot kiss just below my ear. "Been thinking about you all morning."

I shiver, desire pooling low in my belly at his words. "I missed you too," I breathe, tilting my head to give him better access. "I'm so glad you're here."

Ryan runs his hands up my sides, thumbs brushing the sides of my full breasts and making me gasp. He chuckles lowly, the sound rumbling through his chest.

"Let's eat lunch quickly so I can spend more

time showing you just how much I missed you," he suggests wickedly, eyes darkening with lust.

I nod eagerly, biting my lip. My body is already thrumming with need for him. After all this time, I still can't get enough. With a final squeeze, Ryan releases me and I lead him to the counter, our lunches and some private time together awaiting us. I'm so grateful he gave up his stressful city job to be here with me, the sheriff of our quaint little town. I don't know what I'd do without our stolen moments together in my bookshop every day.

We eat quickly, exchanging heated glances and playful banter as we go. I can't wait for him to touch me again, to feel his strong hands on my swollen belly, to hear the filthy things he whispers in my ear. I've come to crave them, crave him, more than I ever thought possible.

As soon as we've finished our sandwiches, Ryan stands, the bulge in his pants evident. He steps closer, circling an arm around my waist and pulling me flush against him. "I can't wait any longer," he growls, his voice a low rumble that sends shivers down my spine.

"Neither can I," I confess with a shy smile. My insides liquify as he lifts me onto the counter, spreading my legs wide. He's always so considerate, even now that my stomach is round with our child.

"I can't believe we're having a little human together," he marvels, running a hand over my belly. "A constant reminder of how much you're mine."

His words send a shiver through me, and I moan as he slides a finger inside me, brushing against my swollen nub. "Ryan," I gasp, arching my back. I'm already on edge, aching for more.

"You like that, don't you, sweetheart?" he asks, his voice a low rumble in my ear.

"I...I do." I can hardly think straight with his skilled fingers teasing me.

"Tell me what you want," he growls, nipping my neck.

My whole body flushes.

"I want you," I whimper, my face flushing.

"You want me to come inside your wet pussy?" His fingers pick up the pace, and I'm already teetering on the edge.

"Y-yes, Ryan!" I cry out as my orgasm crashes over me, wave after wave of pleasure washing over me.

"That's my good girl," he praises, kissing me hard, his tongue invading my mouth as he devours me. I'm a puddle by the time he pulls away, but he's not done with me yet.

Flipping the sign to 'Closed', he scoops me up in his arms and carries me to the back of the store. There, he lays me down on a pile of plush blankets we laid there just for this purpose.

"Spread your legs for me, Ava ." His voice is rough with desire, and I obediently comply.

"I love you, Ryan," I whimper, my eyes heavy with lust as he positions himself at my entrance.

"I love you too, Ava," he says, his voice possessive as he thrusts into me, filling me completely. "Forever and always."

I moan, wrapping my legs around his waist and pulling him closer as we lose ourselves in each other, our bodies moving in perfect harmony.

Ryan places his hand protectively on my swollen belly as he continues to saw in and out of me.

"You're so fucking gorgeous like this," Ryan growls, his hand splayed possessively over my rounded stomach as he drives into me. "All full of my baby, your tits swelling, your body changing. Fuck, it's the hottest thing I've ever seen."

I moan wantonly, my head thrashing against the blankets as pleasure consumes me. The way he's talking, the raw need in his voice, it sets my blood on fire. "Yes, Ryan," I whimper. "I'm all yours. This body is all for you."

"Damn right it is," he snarls, snapping his hips harder, his cock hitting that secret spot inside me that makes stars explode behind my eyes. "This sweet cunt belongs to me. I'm gonna fill you up again and again until you're carrying another one of my babies."

"Please," I beg shamelessly, too far gone to care how desperate I sound. "I want it, I want you so deep. Breed me, Ryan."

He makes a harsh sound, almost like a roar, and then he's pounding into me, ruthless, relentless. One hand still clutches my belly while the other finds my clit, rubbing hard circles. "Come on my cock," he demands roughly. "Squeeze the cum out of me with this greedy pussy."

His filthy words are my undoing. I detonate with a silent scream, my walls clamping down on him like a vice as ecstasy crashes through me. Ryan follows me over the edge with a shout, his hips churning as he spills inside me, painting my womb with his seed.

"Jesus, Ava," he pants after, resting his sweaty forehead against mine. "The way you give it up to me... Fuck, baby, you're perfect."

"I can't help it," I laugh breathlessly, cupping his

stubbly cheek. "You turn me into a needy mess. I'd happily let you put a baby in me every year if it means I get to have you like this forever."

"You've got yourself a deal, sweetheart," he rumbles, catching my lips in a deep, sensual kiss. "I plan to spend the rest of my life worshipping this body and keeping you barefoot and pregnant."

I sigh happily into the kiss, my heart so full it could burst. I never imagined I could have a love like this, so all-consuming and passionate. But Ryan stormed into my life and claimed me so completely, I can't remember what it felt like not to be his.

As he starts to harden inside me again, ready for round two, I send up a silent prayer of thanks that this incredible man is mine and that this is my forever. Lazy afternoons in my bookshop, making love and making babies, with the person I cherish most in this world. I couldn't ask for anything more.

Want a free book from Emma Bray? Go to www.authoremmabray.com.

* * *

Keep reading for an excerpt from Tennessee Whiskey.

Nick

I roll down the window and breathe in the scent of freshly mown grass as I speed down the old state highway that now looks like some sort of backwoods backroad. Although it's humid and hot as hell in the southern atmosphere, the fresh, earthy smell of Tennessee is starting to put me in a slightly better mood. Just a little bit.

It sure beats the mechanical, polluted smell of Boston anyway.

The reporters. Always in my face, trying to twist anything into a scandal. Starting rumors.

Yeah, it's no wonder I have a permanent scowl on my face.

Of course, I still kept my house in the city, but it'll be nice to have this country house to get away to when I want a break, and I'm in desperate need of one right now.

As the owner of one of the biggest software companies on the globe, I can work from wherever

I want. Yeah, there are certain meetings I have to conduct in person in the city, but there's no reason why I can't conduct some of them virtually too. The hell away from everybody.

And I gotten this mansion in Tennessee for a steal. What would normally be a thirty million dollar home in Boston I got for a mere two million. Not like I'm lacking in finances. I'm one of Boston's most eligible billionaire bachelors—a moniker than makes me scowl just thinking about it—but I'm a smart investor if nothing else, so I couldn't pass up on the deal when I came across it.

I've never lived in the country before. I was born in the city—with concrete under my feet and all that—but my folks were from around here, so I have some sort of relations in the area even if I've never explored them. Maybe it's time I connect with my roots and slow it down a bit. Get a breather from the hustle and bustle of the city.

I only wish my parents were here to share in my success. They died in a car crash when I was a teen, so they never got to see my rise to billionaire status, and they weren't here for me to buy them the home of their dreams in their hometown, so I guess I'm doing this partly in their honor.

I reach over to flick on the radio and grimace when the twang of country music filters through the air. I hurry to change the station. I might long for the solitude and beauty of the countryside, but that doesn't mean I enjoy the whining that is country music. My tastes are much more refined. I finally find a station playing some light instrumental and leave it there.

When my eyes flick back up to the road, I slam on the brakes with a curse and skid to a stop.

A young woman stands fearlessly in the middle of the road with her hand held up to stop traffic. Granted, I'm the only traffic around. There are no other cars on this otherwise deserted road, but still. Jesus, I could have run her over.

My chest heaves with the adrenaline of my heart jumping up into my chest in panic at the close call, but the girl seems unconcerned. Her fiery red hair curls all around her face and shoulders like a lioness' mane before falling down to her waist. It's unruly and wild, making her look like something untamed.

My eyes rove over her slim frame, from the baby blue tank top and faded cut-off shorts to the thin, tan-colored flip-flops on her feet with red-painted toenails.

I watch in fascination as she bends down and picks something up out of the middle of the road.

When she straightens, I see what's held in her hand and give an incredulous bark of laughter.

A turtle. The girl risked her life to stop traffic and help a turtle cross the street.

I watch as her long legs walk deftly to the other side of the road where she sets the terrapin down on the grass well off the side of the pavement before giving his shell an affectionate pat. She stands and starts to cross the road again to get back into the beat up-looking white truck I've just now noticed sitting on the side of the road.

I lean out of my rolled-down window, "Seriously? You realize I could have run you over?" I ask her with a growl, irritated that she put her life at risk in such a way.

She pauses by my luxury rental car and looks into my eyes for the first time.

Her eyes are a cerulean blue, a stunning color combination with her red hair. Her skin is flawless and milky, not tan like I'd normally expect of southern girls. Her lips are pink and lush, and I can't stop the visceral and immediate reaction of my body to the whole package of her looking at me directly like this.

She's stunning, but it's more than that. Something I can't put my finger on. Something that causes my chest to squeeze and renders me incapable of tearing my eyes from her.

She shrugs down at me like the fact that she endangered herself so recklessly is no big deal. "He needed help," she states simply, her voice smooth and musical and utterly feminine and innocent at the same time.

Her nonchalant attitude snaps me back to the matter at hand. I frown at her. "Nevertheless, that was dangerous."

She frowns. "He's an innocent animal. Somebody had to save him from assholes like you who come speeding down the highway like a bat out of hell. I couldn't just let him get run over."

I blink at the dressing down she gives me and regard her curiously. I can't remember the last time someone talked to me that way. Even the city's most powerful men know better than to show me such disrespect. "You have no sense of self-preservation, do you?"

Her eyes flash at the reprimand, and she crosses her arms over her chest as she points out, "Standing here arguing this point with you is keeping me in the middle of the road."

I realize she might have a point there. She raises a delicate brow at me. I'm stopped in the middle of the road, detaining her from getting back into her shitty-looking truck and getting out of the potential line of traffic.

"Get out of the road," I order her, waiting until she frowns but moves to do as I say before I maneuver my car onto the side of the road behind her truck.

She stops with a hand on the door handle to her truck and looks back at me as I just sit there watching her. I think I might be freaking her out, but I just want to make sure she gets in her vehicle okay and that the piece of shit starts.

It looks dubious at best.

I make a motion at her through my windshield, urging her to go on, and her pretty little lips turn down into a scowl, obviously put off at a complete stranger like me ordering her around. I feel my lips twitch. She's a firecracker. In every way, from her sassy little attitude to that captivating mane of red hair.

I watch patiently as she yanks on the door of the truck and then climbs up into the vehicle that looks way too big for a cute little thing like her.

If she were mine, I'd have her driving a sleek little Mercedes that would complement her but still provide plenty of safety.

She'd be wearing designer labels that would do her figure justice. I'd cover her with aquamarine diamonds that would only bring out the blue of her eyes.

My hands tighten on the steering wheel with the clarity of the images my mind conjures.

I don't know anything about this girl, but she looks like she should be *mine*.

I frown as I hear the turning of her truck's engine before it craps out. The fucker won't start. Just as I suspected. I honestly don't know how she drove it here in the first place. The piece of junk looks like it was on its last leg ten years ago.

I put my car into drive and pull up right beside her before putting it back in park. The window to the truck is rolled down. If I had to guess, I'd bet my last million it doesn't have working air conditioning in it. She eyes me suspiciously as I roll down the passenger side window before nodding to the seat next to me, "Get in," I tell her.

She stares at me from the inside of the truck before she scoffs, "Uh, yeah, no way, buddy."

———

Daisy

I watch his jaw tense as I tell him there's no way I'm getting into his car with him. He might be the most breathtaking man I've ever seen, but I don't know hide nor hair about him, and even the devil was supposedly God's most beautiful angel—that's what my gran says anyway.

His hair is dark and carelessly tousled in a stylish way. His arms look muscular beneath the dark button-up shirt he's wearing, the sleeves rolled-up to reveal strong forearms and a few buttons undone to reveal the top of his chest.

My heart thumped in my chest when he first spoke to me so moodily. A strange warmth filled my body at the deep timbre of his voice, but it was quickly tempered with annoyance at his sharp tone, ordering me about as if I'm a child.

Perhaps the most arresting thing about him, though, is his golden eyes. They're not brown, and they're not exactly amber. They're the most unique hue I've ever seen—in eyes anyway. They glimmer at me beneath his dark brows now as he frowns at me.

I think all the man knows how to do is glower and frown.

And order me around.

And treat me like I'm stupid for caring about the sanctity of animal life.

He curses, "I can't very well leave you here stranded."

"Don't worry about me," I retort back at him through our windows. "I'll be fine."

He runs a hand through his hair as he turns his head to glance out his sideview mirror before he suddenly slams his car into gear and shoots up in front of my truck, pulling his car into park off the side of the road in front of me.

I'm glued to the spot in shock as I watch the driver's side door open and see him step from the fancy vehicle with a long unfolding of limbs.

I gulp as he slams the door of his car shut and starts stalking over toward where I sit in my truck. My piece of crap truck that *would* choose today of all days to act up on me. I shouldn't have turned it off when I stopped to help the turtle cross the road. I should have just left it idling. I knew better. I knew that sometimes my ornery truck refused to start. Stupid, stupid, stupid!

I suddenly realize the danger of my situation. I'm stranded on the side of the road with a total stranger. My dumb self forgot to grab my cell phone before I left the house, something that I do frequently. I never really worry about it, though, when I'm just going to see my gran. She's about a seven-minute drive from where I live with my parents.

I consider jumping out of my truck and

running. Maybe that would be the sensible thing to do, but I'm too stubborn and have too much pride to run. If the devil is coming for me, I'll meet him head on, and I sure as hell won't go down without a fight.

I sit up straighter in my seat and glare at the man defiantly as he finally reaches my truck.

He leans into my truck with an arm on the top of the window, his golden eyes boring into mine, seeming to burn me with their heat at such close range.

My breath catches in my throat despite myself. Instead of feeling fear, though, as I probably should, I feel this keen sense of excitement.

He stares at me for a long moment. I feel his eyes scorching every inch of my skin as they travel over my face. The intensity in his gaze is unnerving, like he's trying to see deep inside me to my soul.

"I just want to make sure you get home okay." His eyes seem to soften, and he suddenly looks more approachable, less brooding.

I still don't trust him for a minute.

"You're not from around here, are you?" I don't know why I ask it. It's obvious he's an out-of-towner. Everybody knows everybody around here, so the fact that I've never seen the guy lets me know with absolute certainty that he's not from around here.

And I'd certainly remember if I'd ever seen anyone like *him* before. He looks like one of those guys you see on the movies or the covers of magazines. His clothes look perfectly tailored to him and probably cost more than my parent's monthly mortgage.

His gaze never falters from me, but his lips finally quirk up in the semblance of a smile. Or perhaps it's more of a smirk.

"Not yet," he says by way of answer.

I frown at him, tilting my head to the side as I consider his odd answer. His eyes are still holding mine, but I'm broken from the golden trance of them when I hear the whooshing of a vehicle coming around the corner.

I look up just as I see Jake's brand-new truck rounding the corner. I see the stranger's gaze following mine to the truck, and his frown deepens as it slows when Jake obviously notices my truck sitting on the side of the road.

I feel an odd mixture of relief and disappointment at the appearance of a friendly face who can help me. I don't really know where the disappointment is coming from because there's no way in hell I was ever going to get into a car with this man I don't even know. My childhood friend showing up couldn't have been better timing.

"Daisy!" Jake rolls down his window and yells at me with his boyish grin.

"Daisy," I hear the dark-haired man repeat my name thoughtfully as if he's trying it out for size. I feel his stare on me, but I ignore him and the heat that flushes my face as I call back to Jake, "Hey, Jake!"

"The old girl crap out on you again?" Jake asks me knowingly. Yeah, he's picked me up more than once when my truck wouldn't start.

"Yeah," I nod as I open the door of my truck. The stranger steps back just in time to avoid the swing of my truck door smacking him as I hop out.

I can feel him scowling again, but I continue to ignore him. I'm not purposefully trying to be rude, but Mr. Grouchy Pants has done nothing but stare and glower at me since I met him, and I'm already over it.

I run over to Jake's truck and hop into the passenger side. I see my sandy-haired friend looking at the dark-haired man curiously.

"Who's that?" he asks, making no move to hide his interest in the stranger.

I shrug, not even glancing back at whatever-his-name-is. I feel a pang when I realize I don't even know his name, but then I realize it's probably for the best. He's just someone passing through, and I'll surely never see him again.

"Just someone who stopped to see what was going on."

Jake frowns. "Good thing I showed up when I did then. You don't need to be taking rides from strangers, Daisy," he warns.

"I know," I agree with him. "I wasn't going to."

"I don't think he would have hurt me, though," I can't help adding.

Jake looks at me quizzically, but thankfully he doesn't say anything about my odd comment. Instead, he just nods to the dark-haired guy before he pulls away from the curb and starts off down the road.

I chance a glance in the sideview mirror back at the man still standing by my truck on the side of the road. His jaw is clenched, his eyes boring into us as we drive away, his hands fisted at his sides.

I feel a shiver run up my spine despite the summer heat.

It's definitely a good thing Jake came along when he did.

Get Tennessee Whiskey here: Tennessee Whiskey.